# The Khan's Daughter

❖ ✿ ❖

## A MONGOLIAN FOLKTALE

BY **LAURENCE YEP**

ILLUSTRATED BY
**JEAN AND MOU-SIEN TSENG**

SCHOLASTIC PRESS / NEW YORK

*The Khan's Daughter* is an adaptation of a story translated by Bernard Jülg and published in 1868 in *Mongolische Märchen*.

*Library of Congress Cataloging-in-Publication Data*

Yep, Laurence. The khan's daughter / by Laurence Yep : illustrated by Jean and Mou-sien Tseng. p. cm. Summary: In this retelling of a Mongolian folktale, a simple shepherd must pass three tests in order to marry the Khan's beautiful daughter. ISBN 0-590-48389-7 l. Tales—Mongolia. [l. Folklore—Mongolia.] I. Tseng, Jean, ill. II. Tseng, Mou-sien, ill. III. Title. GR336.M66Y46 1997 398.2'09517'302—dc20 95-25150 CIP AC

12 11 10 9 8 7 6 5 4 3 2 1 7 8 9/9 0 1 2/0 46

Printed in Singapore. First printing, March 1997.

The text type was set in 13 pt. Hiroshige Book.

**About the art:** The jacket painting was executed in acrylic against a gold-leaf background. Other paintings, ornaments, and border frames were executed in watercolor. The ornaments are based on motifs found in Mongolian art.

The musical instrument shown on the previous page is a Mongolian horse-head cello. In traditional Mongolian culture, storytellers often played this instrument as accompaniment to their tales.

The script to the left shows "the Mongol khan's daughter" written in Mongolian characters. Read from top to bottom, it is pronounced "*Mon*-gol ha-*gaan* nee oh-*hun*."

**About the names:** In Mongolian, Möngke is pronounced "*Mon*-kay"; Tengri is pronounced "*Ten*-grih"; Borte is pronounced "Bor-*tay*"; and Bagatur, which means "hero," is pronounced "*Baa*-tar."

To Joanne,
who points the way.
*L.Y.*


In memory of
Aunt Saran, a real
Mongolian princess.
*J. and M.T.*

Along time ago, there was a poor man who told his son, Möngke, that he would become rich some day and marry the Khan's daughter. When his father died, Möngke spent many long, lonely years tending sheep while he waited for his father's words to come true.

Finally he said to himself, "If I stay here any longer, I will surely make my father into a liar. For the Khan's daughter knows no more of my father's prophecy than she knows of me. Perhaps I'd better seek her out." So he drove in his master's flock, put on his coat of red, and set out to seek his bride.

On foot, he crossed the vast, grassy plains that stretched like a great green sea. On and on he walked beneath the bright blue sky of Tengri, the ruler of all things, until he reached the city of the Khan.

Domed tents spread all the way to the horizon like so many buttons sewn onto a giant sheet of brown felt. From their tops rose smoke like threads of cotton waving in the wind. And with the horses were tethered haughty camels and oxen and even big, hairy yaks. Everywhere soldiers and citizens hurried to get ready, for the Khan's great enemy was preparing to invade.

Möngke tried not to stare, but he had never seen so many people in his life.

Remembering his father's prophecy, Möngke marched straight to the great domed tent in the very center. "I am Möngke, and it's my destiny to marry the Khan's daughter."

Inside, the Khan's wife and daughter had been serving the Khan and his captains. When she heard Möngke's claim, the Khan's wife straightened in outrage. "How dare that dog presume such a thing." And she would have ordered the guard to execute Möngke right away.

However, the Khan's daughter, Borte, laughed and reminded her mother, "If a Khan may marry a commoner's daughter, a commoner may marry a Khan's daughter." For Borte's mother had been a commoner before the Khan had married her.

Then the Khan turned to his captains. "Let us amuse ourselves with this bumpkin before we go back to planning the war."

Though she was still outraged, the Khan's wife smiled back at her husband. "Only if you allow me to set three tests for him."

When the Khan agreed, Borte and her mother withdrew behind a rug hung up like a wall.

Möngke felt shabby in his red coat when he knelt before the Khan, who wore gold silk and held a jeweled sword. Behind him sat a fierce falcon and seated all around him were his mighty captains.

Even so, Borte thought he might have possibilities.

However, before she could say anything, her mother whispered to the Khan, "Our daughter's husband must be strong. In the mountains, there are seven demons. Let him fetch back their wealth."

The Khan and Borte believed it a harsh task, but the Khan told Möngke to return with the demons' treasure.

Möngke was afraid. But he had caught sight of the Khan's daughter and would have agreed to anything. "Just point the way."

Because she felt sorry for him, the Khan's daughter baked Möngke seven loaves with sesame seeds and seven without.

But when Borte wasn't looking, her mother poisoned the sesame loaves and presented them herself to Möngke. "Eat the seven loaves with sesame seeds on the way there and the seven plain loaves on the way back." The bread would make an end of Möngke even before the seven demons could.

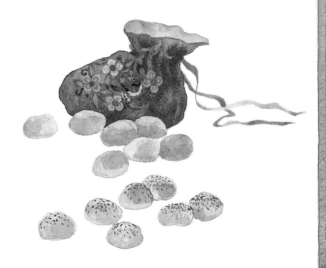

So Möngke rode across the plain and into the mountains on the little horse the Khan had given him. Carefully, he picked his way through the dense forest until he reached steep, lifeless rocks as sharp as knife blades.

The further he rode among the barren crags, the more he wondered about the wisdom of the quest. So, since food always cheered him up, he sat down to eat. But since he hated getting the sesame seeds stuck in his teeth, he ate the plain loaves first.

By then the seven demons had caught wind of him. Sweeping out of their cave, they roared, "Who dares invade our home?"

Terrified, Möngke abandoned his pouch and galloped away.

However, the demons paused when they reached his pouch. Peeking inside, they found the sesame loaves. "One for each of us," they exclaimed in delight. "How thoughtful of the main course to provide the appetizer, too."

But the instant they devoured the poisoned bread, they dropped dead.

In the meantime, though, Möngke had stopped in shame. "What will the Khan's daughter think of a coward?" And so he rode back.

When he found the demons slain, Möngke hauled the treasure back to the Khan.

But the Khan's scouts had brought word that the enemy was invading. And the Khan himself was already donning his armor when Möngke tumbled the demons' treasure at his feet. There were bushels of gold and pearls from China, jade from Khotan, and even fire orbs from far India, for the demons had looted many caravans.

However, before the Khan or Borte could speak, the Khan's wife said, "Our daughter's husband must not only be strong, but he must be brave. Let him drive the enemy from our land."

Though he was even more afraid this time, Möngke sighed, "Just point the way."

So the Khan gave some horsemen to Möngke to lead in advance of the Khan's own army. And Möngke led his little band across the plains until they reached a wooded hill where they decided to rest.

Suddenly the ground shook beneath them, and a scout galloped back. "Our enemies are coming — and there are thousands of them."

Möngke nervously climbed onto his horse. "A dozen or a thousand, we'll drive them away like sheep."

However, his men grumbled, "He knows more about herding than fighting. If we follow this shepherd, we will surely die."

So while his men retreated, Möngke galloped forward — straight into a young sapling. He became so entangled with its branches that he uprooted the entire tree in his mad dash.

When the enemy saw the green-haired warrior plunge out of the woods, they stared. "One . . . five . . . I can't count all of his arms," one soldier said.

Their Khan shook with fear. "It must be one of the seven demons!"

In a panic, they fled, leaving their pack animals behind.

Möngke returned leading the long train of animals loaded down with his spoils. The Khan was amazed to see him, for Möngke's own men had reported that he had died.

Then the Khan and the people could not praise Möngke enough, and even the Khan's wife had to admit that he had proved himself worthy. But Borte interrupted the celebration. "He has met your conditions, but not mine."

This time, Möngke was quite full of himself. "I have vanquished demons and armies. There is nothing I fear."

"And yet," Borte said, "there is always someone stronger and braver and smarter. For your third task, you must conquer Bagatur the Clever and Mighty."

"Just point the way," Möngke boasted, and the next day he set out.

As Möngke rode across the plain, he saw a column of dust. Squinting, he saw a horse, and upon the horse was a rider clad all in black with a scarf hiding the rider's face.

"Who are you?" Möngke demanded.

"I am Bagatur," the rider announced in a gruff voice. "Surrender."

Desperately, Möngke loosed an arrow, but it fell wide of its mark. Then Bagatur sent an arrow whistling past Möngke's ear. "I shot to miss," Bagatur called. "Next time, I won't."

Terrified, Möngke tumbled from his saddle and knelt upon the dirt. "The Khan's daughter tried to warn me, but I wouldn't listen. I have met my match. Mighty Bagatur, take my horse and my armor and weapons, but please spare me."

With a laugh, Bagatur took everything and rode away.

As he stood in rags, Möngke told himself, "You were a fool not to heed the Khan's daughter." He would have gone home, but he wanted to catch one last sight of the Khan's daughter. "One final look will be worth the shame and humiliation," he said, and set out.

After a few miles, Möngke saw Borte sitting in the middle of the plain.

"Have you met Bagatur yet?" she called to him.

Wanting to impress her, Möngke bragged, "I beat Bagatur so badly that I felt sorry for him. So I gave him my arms as well as my horse."

Borte drew a scarf over her mouth and warned in Bagatur's gruff voice, "Speak the truth or face my wrath once again."

Red-faced, Möngke understood that Bagatur had been the Khan's daughter in disguise. "You won, and I lost."

Borte dropped the scarf and smiled. "More than a hero, I want a prudent husband who won't get himself killed at the first opportunity."

"I will always listen to you," Möngke swore. "Just point the way."

"Then," Borte announced, "you have passed the final test. And we will tell no one the truth about your fight with Bagatur."

"Not even your mother?" Möngke asked.

"Especially my mother," Borte said.

Then Borte led him to a gully where she had hidden the horses,
and when they returned to the city, they were married.

The Khan gave Möngke half of everything he owned and treated him as an equal in all things, and Möngke treated Borte the same. And such was their reputation for courage and wisdom that their enemies stayed far away and they lived contentedly for the rest of their lives.